For Brendah Malahleka, who sent the Christmas card – M.H.
For my mother, and in loving memory of my father - L.R.

Three Wise Women copyright © Frances Lincoln Limited 1999
Text copyright © Mary Hoffman 1999
Illustrations copyright © Lynne Russell 1999

First published in Great Britain in 1999 by
Frances Lincoln Limited, 4 Torriano Mews
Torriano Avenue, London NW5 2RZ

British Library Cataloguing in Publication Data
available on request

ISBN 0-7112-1423-9

Set in Stone Sans

Printed in Hong Kong

1 3 5 7 9 8 6 4 2

THREE WISE
WOMEN

Mary Hoffman
Illustrated by Lynne Russell

FRANCES LINCOLN

In the west, the sky was bright with stars as a young woman stayed up late, baking bread. As she waited for the dough to rise, she went to the door and combed her hair, singing a song about the moonlight.

Suddenly she stopped. Far away in the east there was a new star, brighter than all the rest. It was so bright that it bathed the woman's kitchen in star-shine. The beams from the star shone right on to the dough. The woman stared in disbelief – the dough was rising, as if filled with starlight.

She was afraid to touch it at first, but it was quite firm and ready to be baked. So she cooked it in the oven.

"As soon as it is ready," she said to herself, "I shall take the star-bread and travel east. I must find where the great light is coming from."

Way down in the south, where countries are hotter,
another woman sat up late at night rocking her child.
He was cutting a tooth and could not sleep. His mother
hummed to him and loved him with words that no one
else could understand.

"Shall Mama get you the moon, sweet baby?" she
crooned, taking her child out into the night to find
a breeze. "I could cut you a slice like a piece of mango
to cool your poor mouth."

The young child stretched out his fat little arms
to the moon and his mother laughed. Then they saw a
strange sight – a bright new star rising in the north-east.
Starlight shone on the child's face, making him smile.
His mother watched in silence. Her heart filled with
desire to leave her village and follow the bright star.

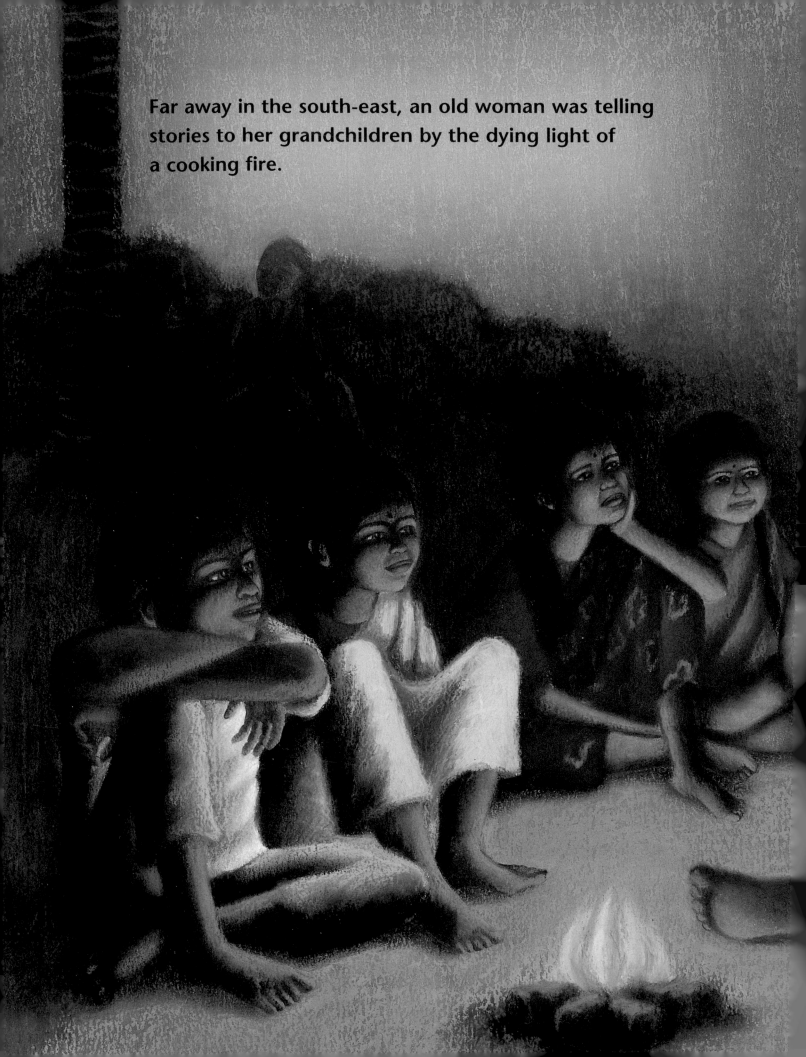

Far away in the south-east, an old woman was telling
stories to her grandchildren by the dying light of
a cooking fire.

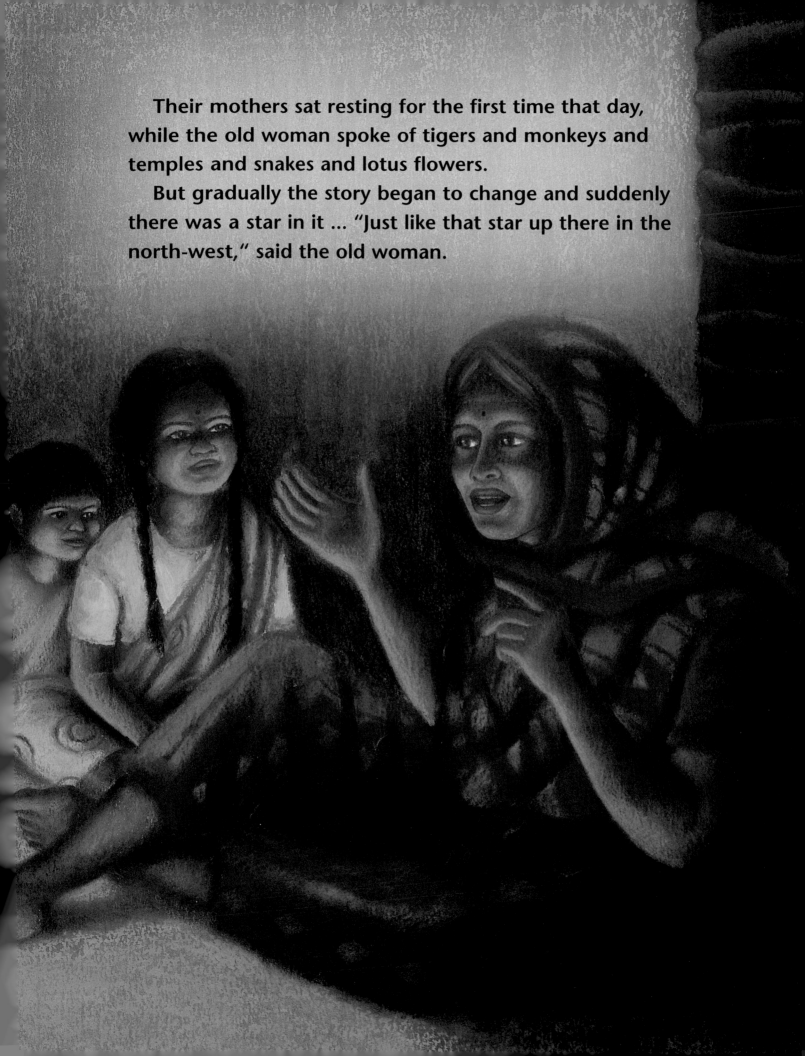

Their mothers sat resting for the first time that day, while the old woman spoke of tigers and monkeys and temples and snakes and lotus flowers.

But gradually the story began to change and suddenly there was a star in it ... "Just like that star up there in the north-west," said the old woman.

"Then what happened, Grandma?" the children
prompted her, for she had stopped in mid-story and
was gazing at the star, till it filled her mind. And all
the children hushed, and gazed with her, forgetting the
story they had been listening to and wanting a new one,
full of silver starlight.

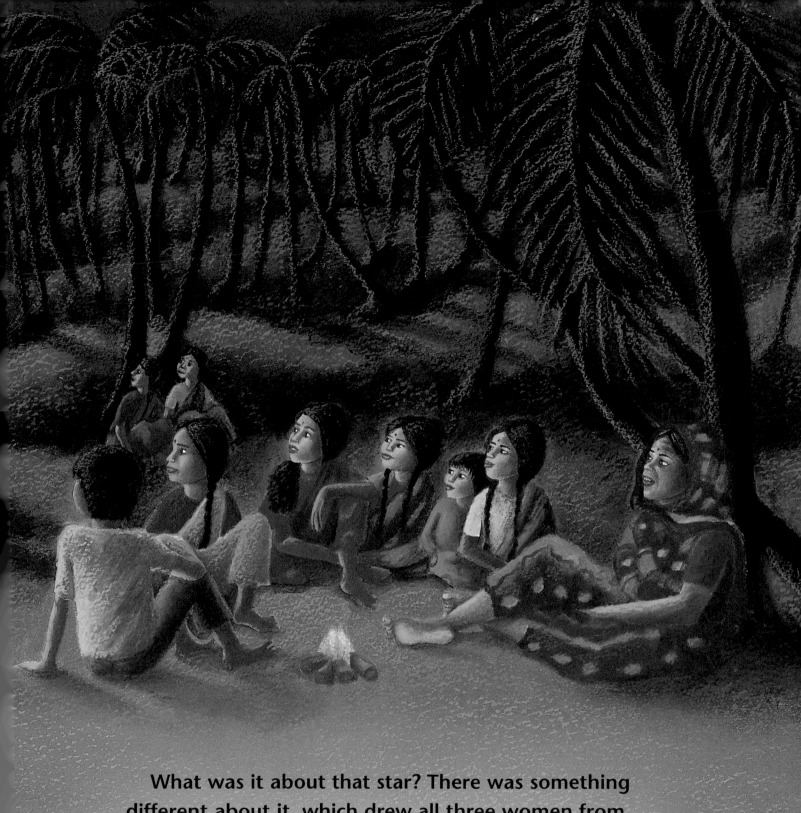

What was it about that star? There was something different about it, which drew all three women from their homelands; and something the same, that said to each of them, "Follow me."

They met on a path of starlight, not knowing how
long or far they had travelled. They were not hungry
or thirsty or tired, so each supposed her journey had
been short.

They found themselves on a dusty road at midnight,
where the sky was a deep dark blue and the moon
a fingernail of mother-of-pearl.

Each woman looked towards her own bright star,
which seemed to stand still over a huddle of houses.
   "The end of our journey," said the grandmother.
   "Let me carry your baby for a while," said the
young woman to the mother. And they all walked
together through the hills, past sleeping shepherds,
down to the town.

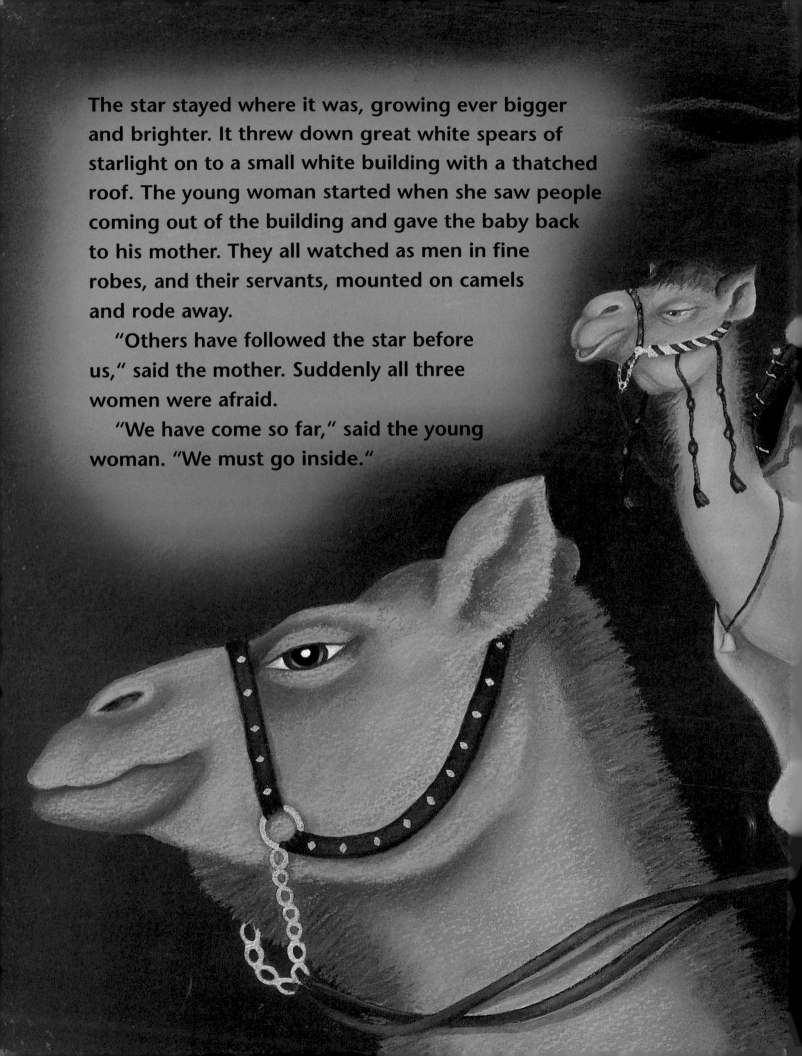

The star stayed where it was, growing ever bigger and brighter. It threw down great white spears of starlight on to a small white building with a thatched roof. The young woman started when she saw people coming out of the building and gave the baby back to his mother. They all watched as men in fine robes, and their servants, mounted on camels and rode away.

"Others have followed the star before us," said the mother. Suddenly all three women were afraid.

"We have come so far," said the young woman. "We must go inside."

They ducked their heads under the low door-beam and looked in. It was just a stable, with horses and donkeys. But it was also a home for a new family, a man and a woman and a newborn child all bathed in silver starlight. And there was gold too, a whole heap of it by the baby's makeshift crib, and other rich presents – but nothing was as rich or as bright as the glow surrounding the baby.

"Come in," said the new mother, and the women entered quietly. Their hearts were full. They too wanted to give presents.

They told the baby's mother how they had left their homes drawn by the star. They had travelled by star-path and moonlight, hardly knowing how they got there.

The young woman took the loaf of star-bread
from her bundle. It was still warm and smelled fresh.
She gave it to the baby's mother and, although he
was too young to eat it, the baby touched the loaf,
as if to bless it.

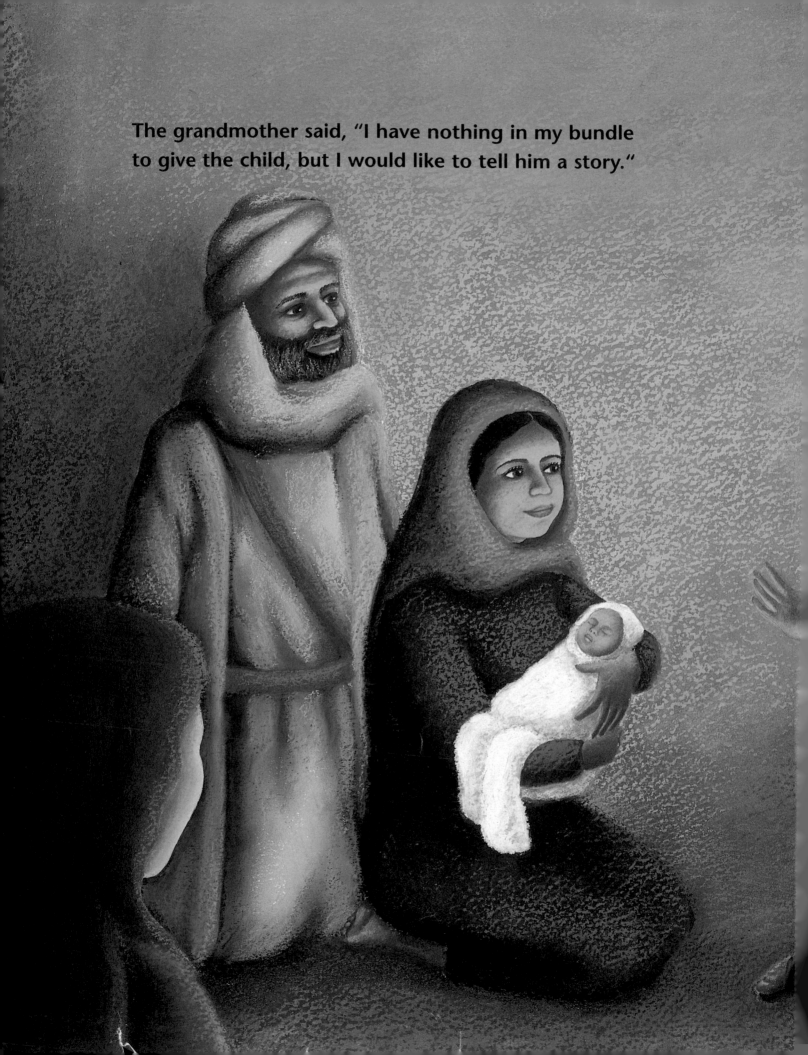

The grandmother said, "I have nothing in my bundle to give the child, but I would like to tell him a story."

Then the three women sat in the straw with the new family and the grandmother told a story full of starlight and hope.

And all the time, the mother from the south held her sleeping baby, and her heart was pounding, for he was all she had to give. And though she was filled with a strange new love for the baby in the crib, her own child was as dear to her as life itself.

When the story ended, her child awoke. Straight away, he saw the baby and held out his arms to him. The two mothers held their sons and the child gave the baby a kiss, full of starlight.

His mother sighed and held her child tight. There had been a present after all.

The three wise women left the stable and walked the paths
the star had made to lead them home. When they got
back to their villages, no one noticed that they had been
away. And no one remembered the star.

But the star-baby in the stable never forgot the women
and their three presents. When he grew up, he showed
that fresh-baked loaves taste even better when they are
shared. He told the most wonderful stories to anyone
who would listen. And the man whose birth had been
marked by a new star taught the whole world that
the greatest gift of all is love.